ONCE UPON
A
JEWISH HOLIDAY

ONCE UPON
A
JEWISH HOLIDAY

by
BEA STADTLER

stories by
Bea Stadtler
and
Shirley Simon

illustrations by
Bill Giacalone

KTAV PUBLISHING HOUSE INC.

ACKNOWLEDGMENTS

Rabbi Pincus Goodblatt for permission to use an experimental edition of *Once Upon A Jewish Holiday* in the religious school of Beth Shalom.

Rose Kumin Rosenwasser whose suggestions, encouragement, and inspiration had been most helpful.

The Methodist Publishing House for permission to use *The Succah and The New Friends* adapted from *Booth for Joel* which appeared in *Trails for Juniors,* October 7, 1956 and copyrighted in 1956 by Pierce and Washbaugh (The Methodist Publishing House),

and

The Lost Chanukah Top adapted from *Dreidel* which appeared in *Pictures and Stories,* December 29, 1957, January 5, 1958 and copyrighted 1957 by The Methodist Publishing House.

Design and Art Supervision by
EZEKIEL SCHLOSS

TABLE OF CONTENTS

מִשְׁפָּחָה

FAMILY

אִמָּא

MOTHER

אַבָּא

FATHER

צִפּוֹר

BIRD

OUR FAMILY

Here is the Cohen מִשְׁפָּחָה .

The youngest Cohen is Miriam. She is three years old.

Next comes Ruth. Ruth is seven years old. She is in the second grade. Every Sunday Ruth goes to Sunday School. Ruth loves to draw and paint.

Dan is the big brother. He is nine years old. Dan is in the third grade. Dan also goes to Hebrew School.

Then there is Mrs. Cohen. The children call her אִמָּא .

Here is Mr. Cohen. The children call him אַבָּא .

Ruth, Dan and Miriam have two pets: a צִפּוֹר whose name is Zippy. She is a talking צִפּוֹר . And a puppy. His name is Kelly. He can do lots of tricks.

שָׁלוֹם

HELLO!

שָׁלוֹם

GOODBYE!

HELLO AND GOODBYE

We say שָׁלוֹם when we meet.

We say שָׁלוֹם when we go away.

שָׁלוֹם also means peace—no fighting.

Dan says שָׁלוֹם to everybody.

Ruth says שָׁלוֹם to everybody.

Even baby Miriam says שָׁלוֹם.

And Zippy says שָׁלוֹם.

Zippy is a very smart bird. So all day long Zippy says שָׁלוֹם. Before she goes to sleep she says שָׁלוֹם. In the morning when she awakes she says שָׁלוֹם.

בֵּית כְּנֶסֶת

TEMPLE

שׁוֹפָר

RAM'S HORN

רֹאשׁ הַשָּׁנָה

NEW YEAR

רַבִּי

RABBI

שָׁנָה טוֹבָה

HAPPY NEW YEAR!

DAN AND THE SHOFAR

Miriam had a toy that looked like a horn. It was a horn. It was a שׁוֹפָר. A שׁוֹפָר is made of a ram's horn. This was the Rabbi's שׁוֹפָר. He left it with the Cohen family when he visited there. Dan picked up the שׁוֹפָר. He put it to his mouth. He blew. Nothing happened. He blew again. Still nothing happened. His face became red. His cheeks puffed out like balloons. Still no sound came from the שׁוֹפָר.

Mother called, "Dan, we must go shopping. We must go shopping for new clothes. We need new clothes for רֹאשׁ הַשָּׁנָה."

"What is רֹאשׁ הַשָּׁנָה?" asked Miriam.

"רֹאשׁ הַשָּׁנָה is the Jewish New Year," said Dan.

"Dan will get new clothes. Ruth will get new clothes. And Miriam will get new clothes," said mother.

12

"What about Zippy?" asked Ruth.

"We will clean her cage for רֹאשׁ הַשָּׁנָה ," said father.

"Hurrah!!' shouted Dan.

"Dan, do not shout," said mother.

"Dan can not help shouting," said Ruth.

"Dan shouts even when he talks," said father.

"I will try," said Dan. "I will try not to shout, but I have a strong voice."

"What do we do on רֹאשׁ הַשָּׁנָה ?" asked Miriam.

"We go to the בֵּית כְּנֶסֶת to pray to God. We will pray for a שָׁנָה טוֹבָה."

Mother saw the שׁוֹפָר. "Oh Dan" she said, the רַבִּי was here. He left his שׁוֹפָר. Put it in your room. You can give it to him Sunday when you go to Sunday School."

The Cohen family went to do their shopping. "Do not forget the apples and honey," said mother.

"Why do we need apples and honey?" asked Miriam.

"We dip the apples in the honey," said mother, "and pray for a sweet שָׁנָה טוֹבָה."

All week Dan was busy in his room. Mother did not know what he was doing. Father did not know what he was doing. Ruth did not know what he was doing. Even Miriam did not know what he was doing. Sounds came from his room. They were funny sounds. Ruth asked Dan, "What are you doing?" Dan would not tell.

On Sunday morning, Dan brought the שׁוֹפָר to school. He gave it to the רַבִּי. Dan said something to the רַבִּי. Ruth could not hear what he said. The רַבִּי

thought and then smiled. Dan ran off, shouting to a friend. "Do not shout," said the רַבִּי, "You have a strong voice."

On רֹאשׁ הַשָּׁנָה the Cohen family dressed in their best clothes. They went to the בֵּית כְּנֶסֶת .

The רַבִּי prayed. The congregation prayed. Dan prayed. Ruth prayed. Mother and father prayed. Even baby Miriam prayed. And the cantor prayed.

Then the רַבִּי picked up the שׁוֹפָר. He wanted to blow it. He tried to blow and blow, but nothing came out. He called to Dan. The רַבִּי said something to Dan. Dan picked up the שׁוֹפָר. He put the שׁוֹפָר to his mouth. His face got red. His cheeks puffed out. He blew the שׁוֹפָר for the congregation. He blew the שׁוֹפָר for Miriam, for Ruth, for mother and father. The רַבִּי took Dan's hand.

" שָׁנָה טוֹבָה " he said. "May you have a שָׁנָה טוֹבָה ."

" שָׁנָה טוֹבָה " said Dan. " שָׁנָה טוֹבָה " said Ruth. " שָׁנָה טוֹבָה " said mother and father and the whole family.

יֶלֶד

BOY

יוֹם כִּפּוּר

DAY OF ATONEMENT

מוֹרָה

LADY TEACHER

יַלְדָּה

GIRL

בֵּית כְּנֶסֶת

TEMPLE

RUTH IS NEVER BAD

"יוֹם כִּפּוּר is our most holy day," said mother. "It is sometimes called the Sabbath of Sabbaths."

"But what do we do on יוֹם כִּפּוּר ?" asked Ruth.

"We go to the בֵּית כְּנֶסֶת ," said mother. "Grownups do not eat any food on this day. We pray in the בֵּית כְּנֶסֶת . We ask God to forgive us. We ask God to forgive us for the thoughtless or unkind things we have done. We think about these unkind things. We promise ourselves to be better."

Ruth hugged mother. "Now I know what יוֹם כִּפּוּר is," she said.

Mother blessed the candles. Father said the prayer over the wine. Dan blessed the bread. Everyone in the family had a piece of Ḥallah. The chicken soup was very good.

"We must finish our dinner soon," said father. "When the sun sets, יוֹם כִּפּוּר will begin."

"I know about יוֹם כִּפּוּר ," said Ruth. "And I know how we can be better. Miriam can be a better יַלְדָּה than she is. She can try to keep her clothes clean. She can stay away from my dolls. She should not take my things."

"Miriam is a very little יַלְדָּה," said mother. "She will learn."

"And I know how Zippy can be a better bird. Our bird has a lot to think about on יוֹם כִּפּוּר." Ruth said. "You are not a good bird" she said to Zippy. "You fly away when I open the cage. Sometimes you bite my hand. And you do not sing or talk when I ask you to."

Father laughed. "I see that the bird has a lot to pray for," he said.

Ruth took a drink of grape juice. "So does Dan," she said. "I know how you could be better," she said to Dan. "You would be a better יֶלֶד if you came to dinner the first time mother calls you. You could wash your face and hands every day. You could do your school work on time. You could . . ."

"Ruth," Dan said to his sister, "You are telling me how I can be better. יוֹם כִּפּוּר is not a time to tell other people how to be better. It is a time to tell yourself how to be better."

"Me?" said Ruth. "I am a good יַלְדָּה. How could I be better?"

"Of course you are a good יַלְדָּה," said mother. Miriam is also a good little יַלְדָּה. The bird is very good. And our יֶלֶד Dan is of course sometimes very good . . . But we could all be better if we tried. Maybe you can think of something you have done that was not kind. If you think hard, you may remember something."

"Perhaps I can," said Ruth.

בַּיִת

HOUSE

לוּלָב

PALM

אֶתְרוֹג

CITRON

סֻכָּה

BOOTH

סֻכּוֹת

SUKKOT

THE SUKKAH AND THE NEW FRIENDS

Dan Cohen stood at the window of the empty בַּיִת. He watched the movers. The movers were moving furniture into the בַּיִת. It was the Cohen בַּיִת. It was their new בַּיִת. Ruth stood next to Dan.

"I hope we will like this בַּיִת," said Ruth. "I hope we will have friends here. On the old street we had many friends."

Dan nodded. "I did not see a single boy or girl on this street," he said.

Most of the Cohens were very happy in their new בַּיִת. Mother was happy. Father was happy. Ruth was happy.

There was a girl next door. Her name was Nancy, and she was in Ruth's class at school. Nancy and Ruth became friends.

Miriam was happy in the new בַּיִת. She had two little friends. They were Jan and Jay. They were twins. They lived across the street.

But Dan was not happy. There was not one boy his age on the street. "I cannot find any friends here," said Dan.

One day father said, "סֻכּוֹת is coming. It is time to build the סֻכָּה. We will build it in the backyard."

Ruth, Dan and Miriam were glad. They loved to watch father build the סֻכָּה. Father let Dan help. Father let Ruth help. Sometimes he even let Miriam help. Father and Dan began to build the סֻכָּה. Ruth found branches and leaves. Miriam brought fruits for the סֻכָּה. Ruth and Miriam tied the fruits to long strings.

Soon Jan came into the yard. He wanted to help too. Then Nancy and Jay came into the yard. They wanted to help. Dan saw three boys coming to the gate. They were in his class at school. "Hello, may we come in?" one boy asked. His name was Bill.

"Sure," said Dan. "You may come in. You may all come in." The three boys came into the yard. They watched father and Dan. Father and Dan were pounding nails into the boards.

"What are you doing?" asked one boy. His name was Martin.

"We are building a little בַּיִת said father. We call it a סֻכָּה."

"What is a סֻכָּה?" asked Charley.

"It is a little booth. We Jews build one every year at this time," said Dan.

"Why?" asked Charley.

Dan and Ruth told Charley all about סֻכָּה .

"When will you put on the roof?" asked Martin.

"We will make a roof of branches and greens," said father. "We must leave spaces. Then we can see the sky and the stars."

Dan hit a board with his hammer. The nail went into the board.

All the boys wanted to help. Father said they could. "This is fun," said Charley. The boys helped father pound nails into the boards. The girls brought more branches and leaves. Ruth and Nancy gave Dan the fruits tied to long strings. Dan and father tied the strings to the branches and poles on top of the סֻכָּה .

More boys and girls came into the yard. They wanted to help too. Soon the סֻכָּה was finished.

"What will you do with this little סֻכָּה now?" asked Charley.

"We will pray here," Dan said. "We will thank God for the harvest of fruits and vegetables."

"We will say blessings over a לוּלָב and an אֶתְרוֹג," Ruth said.

"What is a לוּלָב?" asked Bill. "What is an אֶתְרוֹג?" asked Charley.

"A לוּלָב is a palm branch," Dan said. "We shake it to the North and South and East and West and up and down. This is to show that God is everywhere."

"And an אֶתְרוֹג," added Ruth, "looks like a big lemon."

"What else do you do in the little סֻכָּה," asked Bill. "Do you play in it?"

"No," Ruth told him. "But we eat all our meals in the סֻכָּה."

"Oh, boy," said Nancy.

"That must be lots of fun," said Martin.

Mother came out with cake and milk. The children ate and then went home. "We had fun," said Ruth. "This was a happy day. Now Dan has friends. He has many friends."

"Yes, father," said Dan, "it was a happy day. I had fun. I love to build a סֻכָּה."

"The boys and girls like the סֻכָּה," said Ruth. "They think it would be fun to eat in it."

"I invited some of the boys and girls to have dinner with us," said Dan. "Then they too can eat in the סֻכָּה."

"That's nice," said mother. "How many boys and girls did you invite?"

"About ten," said Dan.

"Oh, no" said Ruth. "I think there were twelve or sixteen."

"Oh!" said mother. She dropped the tray. "How will we get so many into our little סֻכָּה?"

"I never thought of that," said Dan. He helped mother pick up the tray and the plastic cups.

Ruth jumped up and down.

"I have an idea," she cried. "We can invite two children each night, for eight nights. That way, they can all eat in our סֻכָּה."

"That is a fine idea," said mother.

Dan thought so too.

דֶּגֶל

FLAG

רַבִּי

RABBI

שִׂמְחַת תּוֹרָה

REJOICING OF THE LAW

חַזָּן

CANTOR

תּוֹרָה

TORAH

A PRETTY FLAG

Ruth sat in the kitchen. She had a paint brush in her hand. She was painting a דֶּגֶל. Ruth was very careful to paint two straight blue lines. She painted a blue star on the דֶּגֶל.

Miriam sat at the table too. "I am making a דֶּגֶל" said Miriam. "I am painting it blue and white."

Miriam put her brush into the blue paint. She wanted to paint a דֶּגֶל too. Miriam did not paint two straight blue lines. She did not paint a star in the middle. Miriam painted blue all over the דֶּגֶל. She painted and painted. "Look at my דֶּגֶל!" said Miriam.

Ruth laughed. "That is not a דֶּגֶל, Miriam. That is just a big blue blob. Look at my דֶּגֶל. This is a good דֶּגֶל! I will march with it. I will hold it in my hand. I will march with it in the synagogue on שִׂמְחַת תּוֹרָה. I may even win a prize."

Miriam ran to show mother her דֶּגֶל.

At dinner Ruth showed her דֶּגֶל to father and Dan. Miriam brought her דֶּגֶל too. "Me too march," said Miriam.

"Mother," Ruth said, "please do not let Miriam march in the שִׂמְחַת תּוֹרָה parade. Please do not let her march in the temple with that . . . that thing."

Miriam cried.

"You cannot stop her," Dan said. "Let her march if she wants to. It's a free country."

"If she brings that blue thing I will not stand with her. I will pretend I do not know who she is," said Ruth.

"She will march with her own class," said father.

"It's a fine דֶּגֶל ," said Dan.

The next day, Ruth, Dan and Miriam went to the temple with mother and father for שִׂמְחַת תּוֹרָה . When the services began, Ruth sat with her class. Soon the רַבִּי came down from the

pulpit. He carried a תּוֹרָה . Behind him came the
חַזָּן . He carried a תּוֹרָה . Then came Mr. Cohen and
many other men. Each one carried a תּוֹרָה . The חַזָּן
sang. The רַבִּי and the men marched up the aisle.
The children stood up and began to march behind
the men. Ruth was very proud of her beautiful דֶּגֶל .
She held the דֶּגֶל high as she marched.

Round and round went the marchers. They
paraded around the temple seven times. They sang
as they marched. They sang happy songs. They
were happy God had given the Jews the תּוֹרָה .

When the marching was over, a prize was
given for the best דֶּגֶל . Ruth won a prize for her
דֶּגֶל . It was a small תּוֹרָה . Miriam won a prize too.
"Your prize is for the most original דֶּגֶל ," said the
רַבִּי .

"That means 'different,'" said Dan. "You
should be proud of your sister now," he said to Ruth.

All the children had apples and grape juice.

Ruth looked through her תּוֹרָה . Miriam
looked through her book. " שִׂמְחַת תּוֹרָה is fun,"
said Ruth. "Hurray!" said Miriam as she waved
her דֶּגֶל .

מֹשֶׁה

MOSES

עֲשֶׂרֶת הַדִּבְּרוֹת

TEN COMMANDMENTS

תּוֹרָה

TORAH

מִשְׁכָּן

TABERNACLE

33

MOSES AND BEZALEL

מֹשֶׁה sat and thought. He knew that the Jews needed a place to keep the עֲשֶׂרֶת הַדִּבְּרוֹת . He knew they needed a place to pray. Moses said: "Let us build a מִשְׁכָּן . A place where we can pray to God.

מֹשֶׁה wanted all the people to help. He wanted all the people to feel that it was their מִשְׁכָּן . מֹשֶׁה asked the people to bring their gold and silver. All the people brought their gold and silver. They brought animal skins, spices and oil. מֹשֶׁה wanted an expert person in charge of building the מִשְׁכָּן . He wanted someone who could work with gold. He wanted someone who could show the others what to do. מֹשֶׁה chose a man called Bezalel.

Bezalel built a big furnace where the metal was heated. The gold was melted into one big lump. Then Bezalel and the others hammered the gold. They made the gold into a crown for the תּוֹרָה . They made the gold into candlesticks and ornaments for the מִשְׁכָּן . They made an ark for the עֲשֶׂרֶת הַדִּבְּרוֹת . It was beautiful.

Some men went into the forests and cut down

trees. The trees were rare and precious acacia trees. The men sawed the wood into poles and boards. They built the מִשְׁכָּן out of the poles and boards.

The women helped too. The women were weaving and spinning. They made the cloth for the curtains. Then they made the robes for the priests.

Soon the מִשְׁכָּן was finished. All the people were happy and pleased. It was very beautiful. They felt good because they had all helped to build it.

The outside of the מִשְׁכָּן looked like a great big tent. It was covered with skins of animals, dyed red. There were curtains inside. The curtains were dyed blue, purple and scarlet. All the ornaments were made of gold. There was a table with a gold top. There were gold candlesticks. There were gold vases. The everlasting light was a bowl with oil. The bowl was made of gold.

מֹשֶׁה chose priests. He chose his brother Aaron and Aaron's sons. They wore robes of fine linen. They wore breast-plates of gold and precious stones.

מֹשֶׁה went into the מִשְׁכָּן. He thanked God for watching over them. He blessed Aaron and his sons. מֹשֶׁה blessed all the children of Israel. He said a blessing which is used to this day:

"May the Lord bless thee and Keep thee. May the Lord cause His countenance to shine upon thee and be gracious unto thee. May the Lord lift up His countenance upon thee and grant thee peace."

אֲרוֹן-קֹדֶשׁ

HOLY ARK

בֵּית כְּנֶסֶת

TEMPLE

רַבִּי

RABBI

חַזָּן

CANTOR

תּוֹרָה

TORAH

כֶּתֶר

CROWN

THE MYSTERY OF THE MISSING CROWN

"Hello mother," said Ruth as she came into the house.

"Hello Ruth," said mother. "What did you do in Sunday School?"

"We visited a בֵּית כְּנֶסֶת ," said Ruth. "Beth Shalom has no building of its own. We visited the Community בֵּית כְּנֶסֶת . It was very interesting."

Miriam walked in. "I heard you visited a real בֵּית כְּנֶסֶת today," she said.

Ruth nodded.

Dan came into the house. "heard you visited a בֵּית כְּנֶסֶת today," he said. "I wish Beth Shalom had a building."

"Oh, it was fun," said Ruth. "Father drove us to the בֵּית כְּנֶסֶת . But do you know what happened, mother?"

Just then father walked in. "Did you hear what happened?" he asked.

"Ruth was just trying to tell us something," said mother.

"Well," said Ruth, "the רַבִּי showed us a beautiful תּוֹרָה. In fact, there was more than one תּוֹרָה.

Each תּוֹרָה had a mantle on it. One תּוֹרָה had a mantle of dark red velvet. One mantle was of dark blue velvet. One mantle was of dark green velvet. Each תּוֹרָה had a beautiful כֶּתֶר. The one with the blue mantle had a silver כֶּתֶר. The one with the

red mantle had a gold כֶּתֶר. But the תּוֹרָה with the green mantle had no כֶּתֶר at all. I asked why this תּוֹרָה did not have a כֶּתֶר. רַבִּי Goodblatt did not know. He looked surprised. He looked worried. He called Mrs. Feldman, who was the principal of their school. She did not know where the כֶּתֶר was. He called the חַזָּן. The חַזָּן looked worried. He did not know where the missing כֶּתֶר could be."

Mother was very interested in the story. She even stopped stirring the soup.

Miriam was sitting with her chin cupped in her hands. Her eyes were wide open. "Well, where was it?" she asked.

Dan said, "I'll bet someone walked off with it."

"Oh Dan," said father.

Ruth continued. "The חַזָּן opened the אֲרוֹן־קֹדֶשׁ so that we could see how the inside of it looked. All the children were too frightened by the missing כֶּתֶר to get too close. But not me," said Ruth proudly. "I was not afraid. I looked in.

The whole אֲרוֹן־קֹדֶשׁ was lined in light blue velvet. I put my hand in the אֲרוֹן־קֹדֶשׁ to feel the velvet. Suddenly I felt something cold and hard. I pulled my hand away. I was a little frightened. But then I carefully pulled aside the velvet and there was the missing כֶּתֶר.

"Look, look everybody, here is the missing כֶּתֶר," I said.

"Hurray for Ruth," said Dan.

"Heydaad for Ruth," said Miriam.

"Our Ruth," said mother proudly.

"Then I tried to lift it," said Ruth. "It was

heavy. It was solid silver. רַבִּי Goodblatt came over and helped me. 'See,' he said, 'it fell to the floor of the אֲרוֹן־קֹדֶשׁ. It was hidden by the folds of the velvet in the אֲרוֹן־קֹדֶשׁ. Thank you, little girl for finding our beautiful כֶּתֶר.'"

"I'll bet רַבִּי Goodblatt was proud of you," said father.

"Yes, and Mrs. Feldman patted me on the head. Then רַבִּי Goodblatt explained to us about the beautiful Ner Tamid, the everlasting light. He told us about the beautiful carved doors on the אֲרוֹן־קֹדֶשׁ and about the Ten Commandments that were carved into the doors.

"We all looked at the Sidur. That is a Hebrew book which has prayers in it. We all looked at the Kiddush Cup from which the חַזָּן drinks his wine on Friday night and Saturday morning. It is much bigger and prettier than ours."

"Well," said mother, "you've had a very exciting day, little Ruth. We are very proud of our girl with the bright black eyes. You solved the mystery of the missing כֶּתֶר, Ruth Cohen."

שַׁבָּת

SABBATH

נֵרוֹת

CANDLE

חַלָּה

TWIST BREAD

קִדּוּשׁ

SANCTIFICATION

שַׁבָּת שָׁלוֹם

GOOD SABBATH!

SHABBAT SHALOM

שַׁבָּת is coming. "Dan," said mother, "Please go to the supermarket and buy a חַלָּה."

"I will stop on my way home from school," said Dan.

Ruth and Dan went to school together. "Don't stop for a חַלָּה, Dan," said Ruth. "We learned how to make חַלָּה in Sunday School. I will make a חַלָּה today."

"Okay," said Dan, "Then I will have some time to play baseball before I get dressed up for שַׁבָּת."

When Ruth came back from school, mother was not home. She had gone away with Miriam. Ruth went to work in the kitchen. She set the table with plates and the silverware. She put the נֵרוֹת on the table.

Now and then Ruth would look in the oven to see if her חַלָּה was done.

Then Dan came into the house. "Dan, put the napkins on the table," said Ruth.

"Say 'please'," said Dan.

"Please," said Ruth.

"Okay," said Dan. "Ruth, did you bake a חַלָּה ?"

"Of course," said Ruth. "It is baking now."

Dan sniffed. "It does not smell like the חַלָּה mother bakes" he said.

"Well, what do you expect?" asked Ruth. "I am only a little girl."

Soon mother came into the house with Miriam. "The table is beautiful," said mother.

"Ruth set it," said Dan.

"Dan helped," said Ruth.

"Dan, did you buy the חַלָּה ?" asked mother.

"No, he did not, but we have a surprise for you, mother," said Ruth.

Soon it was time for dinner. Everyone sat at the table. Mother lit the נֵרוֹת . Father sang the קִדּוּשׁ .

"And now," said Ruth, "my surprise." She brought out her חַלָּה. It was a beautiful חַלָּה. It was still hot. There was only one thing wrong with it. It was made of clay.

"Oh, dear," said mother. "Ruth, are you trying to be funny?"

"No," said Ruth. "This is how we make חַלָּה in Sunday School."

"But you can't eat a clay חַלָּה," said mother.

Ruth began to cry. "I guess you can't," she sobbed.

"Don't cry," said father.

"Don't cry," repeated mother.

"Please don't cry on שַׁבָּת," said Miriam.

"Don't cry, Ruth, you will spot the tablecloth," said Dan. "I will go over to Mrs. Norr's house to borrow some חַלָּה from her.

And he did. Then they had plenty of חַלָּה for שַׁבָּת.

"שַׁבָּת שָׁלוֹם" said father.

"שַׁבָּת שָׁלוֹם" said mother.

"שַׁבָּת שָׁלוֹם" said everyone.

"שַׁבָּת שָׁלוֹם" sniffed Ruth.

סְבִיבוֹן

DRAYDEL

חֲנֻכָּה

FEAST OF LIGHTS

מְנוֹרָה

MENORAH

לְבִיבוֹת

PANCAKES

נ ג ה שׁ

NUN, GIMEL, HAY, SHIN

THE LOST ḤANUKAH TOP

"Kelly," said Dan, "stop climbing into the box with the decorations."

Kelly barked.

Dan was putting up the חֲנֻכָּה decorations. Ruth was cutting out a מְנוֹרָה. Miriam was making a סְבִיבוֹן. The Cohen family was getting ready for חֲנֻכָּה. In a little while it would be time to light the מְנוֹרָה. The holiday of חֲנֻכָּה was coming.

"Ruth," said Dan, "please get Kelly out of here. He is spoiling the decorations."

Ruth clapped her hands. "Scat," she cried. The

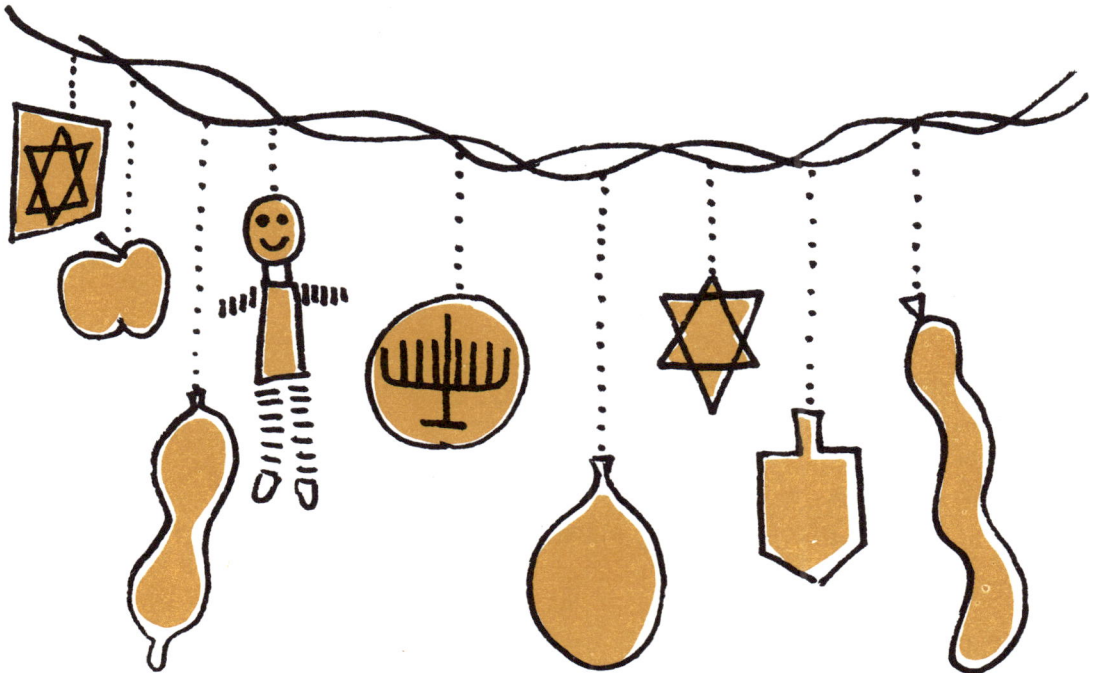

puppy ran off. Then Ruth helped mother. She peeled potatoes for לְבִיבוֹת. She took the מְנוֹרָה off the shelf. She cleaned and rubbed the מְנוֹרָה. Soon the מְנוֹרָה was shining.

It was almost time for Grandma and Grandpa to come. "I cannot find my red סְבִיבוֹן," said Ruth.

"Here is a blue סְבִיבוֹן with gold letters," said Dan.

"No," said Ruth, "That is Miriam's סְבִיבוֹן. My סְבִיבוֹן is red with blue letters."

"You may use my סְבִיבוֹן" said mother.

"Oh no," said Ruth. I must play with my own סְבִיבוֹן. It brings me good luck. I win most of the pennies with my סְבִיבוֹן."

But they could not find Ruth's סְבִיבוֹן. Grandpa and Grandma came. They liked the חֲנֻכָּה decorations. They liked the shiny מְנוֹרָה. "Soon it will be time to light the מְנוֹרָה" said father.

"I cannot find my סְבִיבוֹן," said Ruth. "I have looked through the whole house."

"I see a סְבִיבוֹן under the chair," said Grandma.

It has four Hebrew letters on it. It has שׁ ה ג נ.

Ruth nodded her head. "Yes, Grandma. If it
has שׁ ה ג נ   it is my סְבִיבוֹן."

Dan laughed. "Every סְבִיבוֹן has a נ ג ה שׁ.
And besides, that one is mine. My סְבִיבוֹן is green.
After supper, Ruth, we will all help you look for
it."

Soon they were all at the table eating the
potato לְבִיבוֹת that mother had made. "I love

potato לְבִיבוֹת ," said Miriam, rubbing her tummy.

After supper, the מְנוֹרָה was lit. Father said the blessings. Then the family sang songs, and opened their presents. Each of the children had a very nice present. Even Kelly got a present. It was a rubber bone. "Here, Kelly, come get your present," said Ruth.

"That's funny," said mother. "Kelly always comes right away. He has been too quiet."

"I think he has a bone," said Grandma. "I saw him chewing something red."

Ruth laughed. "A red bone!" she said. Then she thought of her סְבִיבוֹן . She ran into the kitchen. Sure enough, the puppy had her סְבִיבוֹן . " Kelly, let me have my סְבִיבוֹן . Here's a rubber bone for your חֲנֻכָּה present."

"Look," said Ruth. "My סְבִיבוֹן is as good as ever. See how it spins?"

"What are we waiting for, children? Let's play סְבִיבוֹן ," said Grandpa.

"My סְבִיבוֹן is spinning fine today," said Dan.
"Mine, too," said Miriam.

Ruth said nothing. She was busy winning all the pennies.

פֵּרוֹת

FRUITS

יִשְׂרָאֵל

ISRAEL

עֵץ

TREE

טוּ בִּשְׁבָט

NEW YEAR FOR TREES

תְּעוּדָה

CERTIFICATE

A TREE FOR TU B'SHEVAT

"I want to plant an עֵץ. I would like to plant it in יִשְׂרָאֵל ," said Miriam.

"It's a long way to יִשְׂרָאֵל , Miriam," said mother.

"She doesn't want to go there to plant the עֵץ ," said Ruth. "She wants to buy a תְּעוּדָה for it."

"How do you plant with a תְּעוּדָה ?" asked father.

"Well, the money is sent to יִשְׂרָאֵל . There they buy an עֵץ . Then on טוּ בִּשְׁבַט all the children in all the schools get to plant an עֵץ ."

"With our money?" asked mother.

"Yes," said Dan.

"What is so important about an עֵץ ?" asked father.

"You get פֵּרוֹת from it," said Miriam rubbing her tummy.

"Miriam, all you ever think of is eating," said Ruth. "An עֵץ also gives us paper for books and things."

"We can build a house from the wood of an עֵץ," said Dan.

"An עֵץ gives shade," said Ruth.

"And," said Dan, "An עֵץ helps drain swamps. This is very important."

Mother agreed. "Both father and I know all about the עֵץ and what it does. We just wanted to know if you knew. We are proud of our children."

For the next two weeks, all the children of the Cohen family worked very hard to earn their money for a תְּעוּדָה.

Miriam wiped dishes. Ruth dusted. Dan washed the car. Finally they all had their money just in time for Sunday morning.

"My תְּעוּדָה will be in honor of me," said Miriam.

"And mine in honor of me," said Ruth.

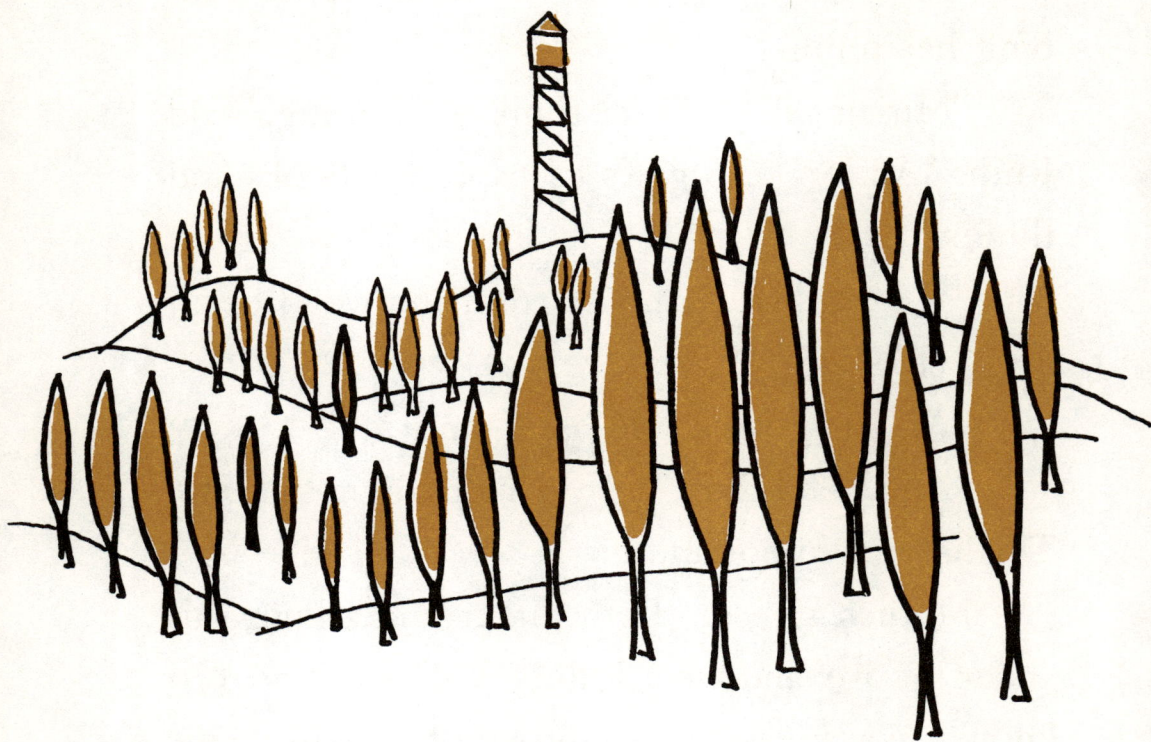

"Not I," said Dan. "I will make mine in honor of someone I love."

"That is a good idea," thought Ruth. "I will also have mine be in honor of someone I love."

Miriam said, "Mine is in honor of someone I love—me."

That day at the assembly, the Rabbi talked to the children about טוּ בִּשְׁבַט . He talked about the bags of פֵּרוֹת all the children would get that morning. He also talked about the עֵץ . He talked about יִשְׂרָאֵל . He talked about how nice it was to give something to someone you love. That we, of Temple Beth Shalom are giving something important to יִשְׂרָאֵל . . . He told them how good it makes you feel inside to be nice to someone. He showed pictures of forests in יִשְׂרָאֵל .

Ruth and Dan felt good. Miriam was sad. She did not feel happy inside. When she went back to her room she said to Mrs. Feil, "I don't want my תְּעוּדָה in honor of me. I want it in honor of someone I love."

The next week each one brought his תְּעוּדָה home. Dan's was in honor of Grandmother Goldstein. Ruth's was in honor of her Uncle Al. Then Miriam showed hers. It was in honor of father and mother. Everyone was proud of her.

Miriam felt happy inside.

עֵץ

TREE

שָׁלוֹם

HELLO!
GOODBYE!

חוֹנִי

HONI

RUTH AND THE JEWISH RIP VAN WINKLE

"Mother," said Ruth one winter day, "we read a story in school that was very interesting."

"Good," said mother, "tell me about it."

"It was about a man," said Ruth. "He slept for 40 years. When he woke up he was an old man."

"Oho," said mother, "I'll bet I know who that old man was. His name was Rip Van Winkle."

"Right!" said Ruth. "Isn't that an interesting story?"

Dan had come into the kitchen as Ruth finished her story.

" שָׁלוֹם," he said.

" שָׁלוֹם," said everyone.

"Ruth," said Dan, "I'll bet you didn't know there is a Jewish Rip Van Winkle."

"You must be joking," said Ruth.

"No," said Dan. "Let me tell you a story about him. His name is חוֹנִי ."

" חוֹנִי " said Ruth, "that is a funny name."

" חוֹנִי , or חוֹנִי the Circle Maker. חוֹנִי used

to draw a circle around him and pray to God that it would rain. Because he was such a good man, God would make it rain."

Ruth and mother were very interested. "But why is he like Rip Van Winkle?" asked Ruth.

"Wait," said Dan, "one day חוֹנִי was walking along and he saw an old man planting a date עֵץ. He laughed. "Old man," he said, "Do you think you will live to see this עֵץ give dates?" The man was not angry. He said to חוֹנִי. "My grandfather planted so that I could eat dates, and I plant for my children and grandchildren."

"The old man was right," said Ruth, "but I

still don't see why חוֹנִי is like Rip."

"Wait," said Dan, "you didn't hear the whole story. חוֹנִי was very tired. He lay down near the date עֵץ and fell asleep. He slept and slept. A kind of wall formed around him. Then one day the wall disappeared and חוֹנִי woke up. He looked around. Beside him he saw a full grown date עֵץ . An old man was eating dates from it. "Old man are you the one who planted this עֵץ ?" asked חוֹנִי .

The old man laughed.

"Dear me, no," he said. "My grandfather planted this עֵץ 70 years ago to this very day."

"Seventy years ago!" cried חוֹנִי . He felt something tickling his chin. חוֹנִי put his hand up to his face and found a long, heavy beard.

חוֹנִי saw that it was snow white. חוֹנִי had slept for 70 years. He was now an old man.

"Your grandfather was a good man," חוֹנִי said to the old man. "He planted for others, and so should we all."

"Poor חוֹנִי ," said Ruth, "he slept even longer than Rip Van Winkle!"

"And woke up even wiser," said Dan.

סַבְתָּא

GRANDMOTHER

צְדָקָה

CHARITY

חֻמָשׁ

FIVE BOOKS OF MOSES

בַּיִת

HOUSE

THE JEWISH WELFARE FUND

Ruth came home from Sunday School. She had a brown envelope in one hand. In her other hand was a note. The note was from Mrs. Stadtler, the Principal of Ruth's Sunday School. The note said that the brown envelope was for the Jewish Welfare Fund.

"What is the Jewish Welfare Fund?" Ruth asked her mother.

"The Jewish Welfare Fund is an organization that helps people. It is an organization for צְדָקָה . Through צְדָקָה it helps people who are sick; it helps others who do not have enough food to eat; it helps people who are old, and it also helps us to get a good Hebrew education. And it helps people in Israel." Mother answered.

"How will I get money for the Jewish Welfare Fund? Will you give it to me?" asked Ruth.

Mother answered, "Oh no, you will have to earn it."

"But if I earn it, I want to spend it. I want to

spend it for candy and ice cream. I need nice new paints."

"That does not sound like my Ruth," said mother. "That sounds like a selfish girl.

Then father said, "Today we will all visit סַבְתָּא Goldstein. She lives in a בַּיִת for old

people." Ruth loved her סַבְתָּא very much. Ruth was glad to go to visit her. She was also glad that she did not have to talk about money for the Jewish Welfare Fund anymore. Ruth clapped her hands. "Yes, let us visit סַבְתָּא ," she said.

They arrived at the בַּיִת for old people. It was a very handsome building. An old man was sitting on the porch. he was reading a book. Ruth asked him: "What kind of a book are you reading?"

The old man looked up and smiled. "This is a חֻמָשׁ ," he said, "the Torah."

They walked into the בַּיִת. סַבְתָּא was waiting for them. She kissed Ruth, Dan and Miriam. She invited the Cohen family to her room.

"You see how pretty it is here," she said to Ruth and Dan. "Look out of the window." The children looked out. There was a garden. It was a lovely garden. There were chairs and a table in the garden. Men and women were sitting in the chairs.

"Yes it is lovely," said Dan.

"Do you like to live in such a big בַּיִת ?" asked Ruth.

"Yes, I like to live here," said סַבְתָּא. "I am happy here. My room is pretty. I have many friends. We take walks in the garden."

That night Ruth said, "I will paint a picture. I will give the picture to סַבְתָּא."

"That is a good idea," said mother. "I know something else you can do for סַבְתָּא Goldstein."

"What is that?" asked Ruth.

"You can help her by giving צְדָקָה money to the Jewish Welfare Fund. When you give צְדָקָה you also help yourself. You feel happy inside."

"But how will that help סַבְתָּא Goldstein?" asked Ruth.

"A lot of money is needed to take care of old people. Most of the money for the the בַּיִת for old people comes from the Jewish Welfare Fund."

"Oh," said Ruth. "I never thought of that. I will try to earn some money this week. I will give it all to the Jewish Welfare Fund. But how will סַבְתָּא Goldstein know I gave צְדָקָה?"

"She won't," explained mother, "because the best kind of צְדָקָה, is when the one who gives does

67

not know where it is going and the one who receives does not know where it came from. That is true צְדָקָה."

מַלְכָּה

QUEEN

מֶלֶךְ

KING

רַעֲשָׁן

NOISE MAKER

מְגִלָּה

MEGILLAH SCROLL

אֹזֶן הָמָן

HAMANTASH-CAKE

פּוּרִים

FEAST OF LOTS

A PURIM TREAT

The Cohen family sat around the table eating lunch.

"I hate פּוּרִים ," said Ruth and pushed back her chair.

"What?" said father.

"What?" said mother.

"No one hates פּוּרִים ," said Dan. I love the מְגִלָּה reading especially.

"I love אֹזֶן הָמָן " said Miriam rubbing her tummy with her hand. I love the רַעֲשָׁן .

"Yes, I hate פּוּרִים ," said Ruth a little louder. I hate the מְגִלָּה and I hate the רַעֲשָׁן .
"I hate the parade. I hate the dress up part. I hate the contest. I hate always losing."

"Aha," said father, "Now it is clear."

"You are a bad sport," said Dan.

"You have to lose some times," said mother as she cleared the table.

"But I lose every year," said Ruth and burst

into tears. "This year I will not even dress up for the contest."

"Too bad," said mother. "The prize is a bike."

"A bike!" Ruth jumped up. Her chair fell over. "Perhaps I will try," she said.

Kelly barked. Zippy said: "Good."

Miriam said, "פּוּרִים is fun."

Ruth went upstairs. She worked and worked

Mother called, "Time for supper."

Dan set the table.

Ruth came down. She said, "In the מְגִלָּה it

says Esther was dressed in a white dress and so—"
Ruth was wearing a white dress. She had made the
dress from an old bed sheet. It was tied with a gold
cord. She walked round and round the table.
Mother and father clapped. Miriam clapped.

"Hurray," shouted Dan. He moved his chair
back to see better.

Zippy said "Good."

Kelly barked and jumped on Ruth. He tore
the dress. "Oh!" wailed Ruth. She began to cry.
"Now I will not try to win the contest! I worked
so hard on this dress, and Kelly tore it."

After supper Dan said, "Ruth, come with
me." Ruth and Dan went away. They whispered
together. They went to Ruth's room. They would
not tell anyone what they were doing.

On Sunday afternoon everyone went to the
temple. Everyone but Ruth. They went to the פּוּרִים
party. They went to hear the מְגִלָּה reading and then
for the פּוּרִים parade. Miriam wore a crown on her
head. She was מַלְכָּה Esther. Dan wore a beard. He

was מֶלֶךְ Ahasuerus. But Ruth did not come. "I will come later," said Ruth.

All the children were dressed up. They all looked like פּוּרִים actors. There were good Esthers. There were bad Hamans. There were beautiful Vashti's. There was even one dressed as a מְגִלָה. There were many who were dressed like Ahasuerus. Each one passed in front of the Rabbi. He sat at a table in front of the room. The רַעֲשָׁן made lots of noise. The Rabbi liked them all.

Suddenly everyone laughed. Then everyone clapped. A real live אֹזֶן הָמָן walked into the room. It walked past all the parents. It walked up to the Rabbi. He stopped the אֹזֶן הָמָן. A little black face stuck out of the huge three-cornered אֹזֶן הָמָן cake.

"Oho," said the Rabbi and stood up from his chair. "A prune אֹזֶן הָמָן."

"I like אֹזֶן הָמָן," said Miriam and rubbed her tummy.

Everyone clapped louder. "I think our אֹזֶן הָמָן wins the prize."

"It's Ruth," said Miriam.

"So it is," said mother and father. Dan just looked pleased.

"Ruth wins the prize," said the Rabbi. He made her stand on the table so everyone could see her.

"I love פּוּרִים," said Miriam and took a big bite of her own prune אֹזֶן הָמָן.

"I love פּוּרִים too," said Ruth.

מָרְדְּכַי

MORDECAI

אֶסְתֵּר

ESTHER

אֲחַשְׁוֵרוֹשׁ

AHASUERUS

וַשְׁתִּי

VASHTI

פּוּרִים

FEAST OF LOTS

הָמָן

HAMAN

QUEEN ESTHER—A PURIM STORY

Long, long ago, in the land of Persia, there was a king. He was called אֲחַשְׁוֵרוֹשׁ . We think this is a funny name, because it sounds like a sneeze.

One day the king gave a big party. Many people came to the party. The king drank many glasses of wine. The wine made him very foolish and loud.

The king roared, "where is my wife? Where is Queen וַשְׁתִּי ?"

Now Queen וַשְׁתִּי was in her room. Her ladies were with her. A servant came to her room. He bowed low.

"The king wants you to come to the party at once," said the servant. "He wants you to come right away."

"I will not come to the king's party," said the queen. "At the king's parties everyone drinks too much wine. Soon all the guests become very foolish and very noisy. It is no place for a queen and her ladies.

The king sent his servant back three times. Each time he asked the queen to come to his party. Each time Queen וַשְׁתִּי said, "No, I will not come."

Then the king said to the servant: "Tell Queen וַשְׁתִּי that she is no longer your queen. From this time on, she is ex-Queen וַשְׁתִּי. Tell her to pack her things and to leave the palace. That will teach her to say 'No' to the king."

Soon after, the king said, "I will choose a new queen. Send messengers all over the land. Find the most beautiful girls. Tell them I will choose a new queen from among them."

Many, many girls came to the palace. Of course each one wanted to be the new queen.

Many miles from the palace there lived a Jewish girl named אֶסְתֵּר. אֶסְתֵּר was kind and good and very beautiful. She lived with her cousin מָרְדְּכַי. מָרְדְּכַי said: "אֶסְתֵּר you should go to the palace. Perhaps the king will choose you as his queen."

אֶסְתֵּר laughed. She did not think the king would choose her. But she went to the palace anyway just to please מָרְדְּכַי.

אֶסְתֵּר did not wear fancy clothes. She did not dress in silks and satins. She did not wear jewelry. אֶסְתֵּר wore just a plain white dress.

The king thought אֶסְתֵּר very lovely. "This girl is beautiful," he said to his servants. "What is more, she looks kind. She looks like a girl who would do as I say. I choose אֶסְתֵּר as the new Queen of Persia."

So אֶסְתֵּר became queen of all the land.

מָרְדְּכַי went to the palace courtyard every day. He wanted to be sure אֶסְתֵּר was safe and well.

One day, when מָרְדְּכַי was in the courtyard, he saw two men acting strangely. He overheard them planning to kill the king. אֶסְתֵּר told מָרְדְּכַי. אֶסְתֵּר told the king. The two men were arrested. A servant of the king wrote down the story of how מָרְדְּכַי had saved the king's life. This servant was called a scribe. He wrote down everything in the king's special book.

King אֲחַשְׁוֵרוֹשׁ had a Prime Minister. His name was הָמָן. He was very wicked. He wanted every man to bow down to him.

One day, מָרְדְּכַי was in the courtyard. הָמָן,
the Prime Minister, came riding by. Everyone
bowed down to הָמָן—well—almost everyone. מָרְדְּכַי
did not bow down. הָמָן became very angry.

"You!" he said to מָרְדְּכַי. "Why do you not
bow down?"

"I cannot bow down to you," מָרְדְּכַי said. "I
cannot bow down to any man. No Jew can bow
down to any man. We can only bow to God."

הָמָן was very angry. "I will fix that Jew
מָרְדְּכַי," he screamed. "I will fix all the Jews. They
will all be hanged."

הָמָן went to see the king. He said: "Oh King
אֲחַשְׁוֵרוֹשׁ, there is a people in this land who are
not true to you. They do not obey the law of the
land. They should be destroyed."

The foolish king did not ask any questions.
He gave הָמָן permission to kill the Jews of Persia.

Soon the news reached מָרְדְּכַי. He ran to
the palace courtyard. He sent a message to Queen
אֶסְתֵּר, telling her of the plans, he begged her to
go to the king and ask the king to free her people.

When אֶסְתֵּר heard this, she put on her most beautiful clothes, and she went to see the king.

The king was glad to see his beautiful queen. He asked her: "Why have you come אֶסְתֵּר? What can I do for you?"

"I have come to invite you to a dinner. Please come and bring הָמָן, the Prime Minister. At the dinner I will tell you my wish."

The king was pleased and said, he and הָמָן would come. הָמָן was happy that the queen had

invited him to a special dinner.

That night the king could not sleep. He called his servant, the scribe.

"Scribe," he said, "please read to me from my special book."

So the scribe read from the special book. He read about how מָרְדְּכַי had saved the king's life.

"Stop!" the king said, "Have we rewarded this man מָרְדְּכַי ? He should have a special gift. He saved my life."

The scribe said that מָרְדְּכַי had not be rewarded.

In the morning, the king called הָמָן , his Prime Minister. " הָמָן ," the king said, "I wish to honor a man who has done much for me. What shall I do for this man?"

Foolish הָמָן thought that the king meant to honor him, he said, "Have the man ride on a beautiful white horse. Give him beautiful clothes. Have someone lead the horse through the streets so that all the people of Persia can see who he is."

"Good," said the king. "The man I wish to honor is מָרְדְּכַי . You, הָמָן , shall lead the horse through the streets. You will cry out, 'This is the man the king wishes to honor.'"

Can you imagine how הָמָן felt? But he had to do as the king commanded.

The next day the king and הָמָן came to the

queen's special dinner. The king was delighted with the dinner. He thought אֶסְתֵּר was very beautiful. "You invited me here for a special reason. Please tell me, and I will do anything you wish, אֶסְתֵּר," he said to his queen.

"Then" cried Queen אֶסְתֵּר, "save my life, oh king. I am a Jewess. Save the lives of my people! There is a man who wants to kill me and my people."

The king became very angry. "Who would dare to do this?" roared the king.

"There he is!" Queen אֶסְתֵּר cried. "There he is! הָמָן!" And she pointed right to the Prime Minister.

What do you think the king did then?

That's right. He ordered that הָמָן should be hanged on the very gallows he had built for the Jews.

Brave Queen אֶסְתֵּר had saved her people.

That is why today we celebrate the holiday of פּוּרִים —the day on which brave Queen אֶסְתֵּר saved the Jews from wicked הָמָן.

פֶּסַח

PASSOVER

הַגָּדָה

HAGGADAH

תִּינוֹק

BABY

אִמָּא

MOTHER

מַצָּה

MATZAH

BABY MOSES IS A LIVING DOLL

Everyone in the Cohen family was getting ready for פֶּסַח .

In Sunday School the children planned to give a play. The play was about תִּינוֹק Moses. Ruth had the part of Miriam, the sister of Moses.

"You will have to bring a doll for the play," the teacher said. The doll will be תִּינוֹק Moses."

At home, the Cohen family was getting ready for פֶּסַח too.

Ruth helped אִמָּא clean the house. Dan helped אִמָּא clean the attic. Even little Miriam helped.

"Soon your cousins will come from Chicago," אִמָּא said.

"They are coming for the Seder," said אִמָּא . "They will stay here during the week of פֶּסַח ."

"There are four cousins," said Ruth, "and an aunt and uncle. We will be very crowded."

אִמָּא laughed. "The more the merrier," said אִמָּא .

We have a הַגָּדָה for everyone.

"Our cousins from Chicago are a pain in the neck," said Dan.

They will disrupt the Seder, said Dan.

"They run around and make noise," said Ruth. "They get into my things and mess them up."

"I don't like them either," said Miriam.

"I think things will be better this פֶּסַח ," אִמָּא told them. "There is a תִּינוֹק now. He is eight months old."

"That will only make things worse," Dan said.

"The תִּינוֹק will cry at night. No one will be able to sleep."

Soon the cousins came from Chicago. They were very noisy. Everyone was crowded. The תִּינוֹק cried at night.

"We are presenting a play for פֶּסַח," Ruth told her cousins. "You may come and see it. I am Miriam."

"Oh, no," said Miriam, "I am Miriam."

"Don't be silly," said Ruth, "I am the Miriam in the play. I am the sister to Moses. My doll will be תִּינוֹק Moses."

"תִּינוֹק Moses is always a doll," said Ruth. "How else can we have a תִּינוֹק Moses?"

"I always thought the doll stuff was pretty silly," said Dan.

"Yes," said the cousins, "a doll for תִּינוֹק Moses. Ha-Ha."

"You all think you are so smart," said Ruth. "If you are so smart, tell me this, what will we use for תִּינוֹק Moses?"

"A תִּינוֹק," said one of the cousins.

"We can use our תִּינוֹק " said another cousin.

So the cousins came to Sunday School. They

brought their תִּינוֹק.   All the cousins were in the play. The big cousins were Pharaoh's soldiers. The baby was תִּינוֹק Moses."

The תִּינוֹק was a fine Moses. He was much better than a doll. He sat up in the basket. He waved his fat little arms. Everyone laughed when the תִּינוֹק crawled across the stage.

When Ruth picked him up, the תִּינוֹק said, "glee goo gah."

After the play Ruth hugged the תִּינוֹק . "This is a תִּינוֹק worth saving," she said. "I am glad that I was Miriam in the play." Ruth gave the fat תִּינוֹק a big kiss.

"We had a wonderful time in your play," the cousins said. And they had a wonderful time at the Seder too. All the cousins helped. They helped Ruth set the table. They helped אִמָּא set out the מַצָּה . They gave everyone a הַגָּדָה .

They helped eat up all the good food.

"We love פֶּסַח food," said the cousins.

We like to read the הַגָּדָה ," said the little cousins.

"We are very glad we came to your house for פֶּסַח," said one of the cousins.

"We are glad you came, too," said Ruth.

"They are very lively," said Dan.

"I love that תִּינוֹק ," said Ruth. "We never had such a fine play at Sunday School."

"The תִּינוֹק was the star," said Dan. This year Moses was a living doll!"

בֵּית הַסֵּפֶר

SCHOOL

מוֹרָה

LADY TEACHER

יִשְׂרָאֵל

ISRAEL

בַּיִת

HOUSE

THE BIRTHDAY

Ruth came running into the בַּיִת. "A holiday is coming. My מוֹרָה says so. And we learned a new song about this holiday." Ruth sang the new song she had learned.

Miriam came running into the בַּיִת. "A holiday is coming. My מוֹרָה says so."

"Did you learn a new song too?" asked mother.

"Oh, yes," said Miriam, "listen . . ." She sang her new song.

Mother thought. Purim is past. Hanukah is past. Shavuot is coming. What can it be?

"It's a birthday," said Dan.

"Whose birthday?" asked father.

"Dan's birthday?" asked mother.

"No," said the children.

"Ruth's birthday?"

"No," answered the children.

"Not Miriam's birthday?"

"No," laughed the children.

"I give up," said mother. "But if your מוֹרָה says so, it must be."

"A birthday, a birthday, a happy, happy birthday," said Miriam.

"It's the birthday of יִשְׂרָאֵל," said Ruth.

"So it is," said mother.

"We will have a party," said father.

"בֵּית הַסֵּפֶר Beth Shalom is going to have a party. A celebration," said Dan.

"What kind of celebration?" asked mother.

"They don't know yet," said Ruth.

"They will have a contest," said Dan.

"The best idea wins a prize," added Ruth.

"I have an idea," said Dan.

"And I have an idea," echoed Ruth.

"Me, too, I have an idea, too," sang Miriam. "Mother will help me write it down."

"Your idea won't be good," teased Ruth.

The next day they dropped their ideas into

the idea box.

At the assembly on Sunday, the רַבִּי told about the program for the birthday of יִשְׂרָאֵל "We had many ideas that children dropped into the box," he said. "But the best idea was . . ." He stopped.

Everyone wondered whose idea won.

"The best idea was from one of our youngest children. בֵּית הַסֵּפֶר Beth Shalom will have a birthday parade. A parade down Taylor Road, with floats."

"Hurrah, hurrah, a parade," everyone shouted.

The רַבִּי raised his hand. "The parade is the idea of Miriam Cohen."

"Hurrah," yelled Miriam.

"My idea of a picnic was not quite as good as yours," said Dan to Miriam.

"And my idea of a special assembly was not quite as good as yours," said Ruth.

Miriam was so happy she pulled Dan's hat off his head.

"We are glad that you won," said Dan and Ruth together. "We are proud of our little sister." They put their arms around Miriam. Mother and father were proud of all their children.

לַ"ג בָּעֹמֶר

LAG B'OMER

סֵפֶר

BOOK

A PICNIC FOR LAG B'OMER

Ruth looked very busy. "What are you doing?" asked Miriam.

"I am making a very special lunch for the ל"ג בָּעֹמֶר picnic," answered Ruth.

"What are you doing, Dan?" asked Miriam.

"I am making a bow and arrow to take to the ל"ג בָּעֹמֶר picnic," said Dan. "After all, every year Temple Beth Shalom has a ל"ג בָּעֹמֶר picnic, and every year mother says, 'Next year you will have a bow and arrow.' This year I am making myself a bow and arrow."

"Well, goodbye everybody. I have something to do too," said Miriam and hurried away.

"What can she be doing?" asked Ruth.

"Not much," laughed Dan.

Ruth picked up the large picnic basket and put it on the kitchen table.

"Here are the sandwiches, the mustard, the pickles, the lemonade. Now, what did I forget?"

"Dessert," called Miriam from the other room.

Kelly thumped his tail under the kitchen table. It sounded like it said "dessert, dessert, dessert, dessert."

Miriam poked her head around the corner. "Whatever you do, don't forget the dessert."

Ruth laughed. "All you ever think about is your stomach," she said.

Miriam came in and stood on her tiptoes to peek under the napkin covering the basket. "Hmm, sandwiches, mustard, vegetables and dessert. Good." Miriam popped a סֵפֶר into the basket, a little golden סֵפֶר.

"What is that for?" asked Dan. "It's not to eat, that's for sure."

"It's a סֵפֶר," said Miriam.

"Silly, I know that," said Dan. "Why are you bringing a סֵפֶר?"

"Well, לַ"ג בָּעֹמֶר is the student's holiday, and I am going to read," said Miriam.

"Read? On a picnic?"

"Don't laugh," said Ruth, "she can read this סֵפֶר."

"And at a לַ"ג בָּעֹמֶר picnic it's all right if I read," added Miriam.

Dan, Ruth, mother, father, Miriam and Kelly were ready to go to the picnic. They got into the car. They drove to the picnic grounds. They greeted all their friends. Then Ruth took her jump rope and ball and went to play with other girls. Dan took his bow and arrow and baseball and went to play with Jerry who was his special friend. Miriam ran over to the swings, but she took her סֵפֶר with her. Mother put the basket under the picnic table. Skippy settled himself under a folding chair. Father and mother went for a walk.

After a while, Miriam got tired of swinging. She took her סֵפֶר and went for a walk. She walked toward the trees. She walked and walked. It was cool. There were many trees. She turned around and

looked back. She could still see the picnic tables.
She walked even farther. On and on she went. She
saw a pretty butterfly. She listened to a bird whistle.
"That sounds prettier than my bird," she said to herself, "He does not really whistle." In front of her,
a little off the path, Miriam saw some pretty red
flowers. She picked one or two. Then she saw some
pretty blue flowers up ahead. She picked a few of
them. Then she decided to go back to the picnic
grounds. She walked and walked. Suddenly, Miriam
knew she was lost. "Mother, Ruth, father, Dan!"
There was no answer. She started to cry. "Don't be

a baby," she scolded herself. She stopped crying and opened her golden סֵפֶר to the first page. She tore a corner from the page and dropped it. As she walked along the path she kept tearing and droping pieces from the pages. She walked this way a long time. Then she was tired. She sat down and read over the pages that were not too torn. That made her feel better. Then she fell asleep under the trees.

All of a sudden she heard someone calling, "Miriam, Miriam! Thank goodness, we have found you." It was mother, and close behind her was father, and Dan and Ruth.

"See," said Dan. "I told you those little pieces of paper on the path were from Miriam's סֵפֶר." He held up the סֵפֶר with the torn pages. "You were pretty smart after all, Miriam, to take the סֵפֶר with you."

"Thanks for saving me, Dan," said Miriam. "Did you save me some dessert?"

Everybody laughed.

"All she thinks about is her stomach," said mother.

"And her סֵפֶר," said father.

יִשְׂרָאֵל

ISRAEL

רוּת

RUTH

שָׁבוּעוֹת

FEAST OF WEEKS

101

GLEANINGS FROM THE CORNERS

The Cohen Family was getting ready for שָׁבוּעוֹת. Dan was decorating the front room with greens and flowers. Mother and רוּת were preparing the cheese blintzes. Father was reading from the Book of רוּת. He read about רוּת and Naomi. He told the children how רוּת left her own land and came to יִשְׂרָאֵל with Naomi. רוּת said to Naomi, "Your people will be my people," and also "your God will be my God." Then father told them how רוּת worked to provide food for Naomi. She worked in the fields of Boaz. Father told them, the people of יִשְׂרָאֵל left grain lying in the corners of the field. This grain was left for the poor.

"That was a very thoughtful custom," Dan said.

"Yes," said father. "It is good to provide for those who have less than we do."

"I like the story of רוּת and Naomi," said Miriam.

"I like רוּת ," said רוּת from the kitchen, "because she was good and loyal. And because I have her name."

"You would," said Dan. He looked out of the window. He saw the postman coming down the walk. Dan ran to the door.

There were three letters for father. One he read out loud to the family. It was from his cousin Malka in יִשְׂרָאֵל . She wrote about her family, her apartment, her work and the weather. She also wrote about an organization for which she did some volunteer work. It was called Keren Yeledaynu, an organization for orphaned children. She sent a picture of a group of children from Keren Yeledaynu. They looked clean but shabby. Malka said they needed clothing.

There was a girl in the picture who looked like רוּת . רוּת studied the picture a long time. Then she went back to helping mother in the kitchen. Soon it was time to put the blintzes into the freezer.

After supper רוּת went into her bedroom. She was there for a long time. When she came out she had a big box. It was filled with skirts and blouses and sweaters.

"What have we here?" asked mother.

"This is for the girls in the picture," said רוּת.

"But here is your favorite sweater," said mother. "It took you a long time to save the money for this."

"It is easy to give things that you don't wear

any more, or that are too small for you," said רוּת,
"but it is harder to give something you really like.
I want her to have something I really like. Anyway,
the rest of these things are either too small or are
things I never wear anymore."

"You might say," רוּת added, "that these are
from the corners of my closet."

"רוּת is like the רוּת in the Bible," father said.
"She knows we should leave some of our posses-
sions in the corners, like the grain left in the fields,
for those in need."

"רוּת is a good kid," said Dan.

רוּת beamed. Dan, like most brothers, hardly
ever praised her. She was very pleased. "I am going
to telephone my friends," she said. "Perhaps they
can give something to the children of Keren Yeledaynu — from the corners of their closets."

TRANSLITERATION DICTIONARY

OUR FAMILY

מִשְׁפָּחָה

FAMILY

MISHPAḤAH

אִמָּא

MOTHER

EEMAH

אַבָּא

FATHER

ABAH

צִפּוֹר

BIRD

TZEEPOR

HELLO AND GOODBYE

שָׁלוֹם

HELLO!
SHALOM

שָׁלוֹם

GOODBYE!
SHALOM

DAN AND THE SHOFAR

בֵּית כְּנֶסֶת

TEMPLE

BET KNESSET

שׁוֹפָר

RAM'S HORN

SHOFAR

רֹאשׁ הַשָּׁנָה

NEW YEAR

ROSH HASHANAH

רַבִּי

RABBI

RABEE

שָׁנָה טוֹבָה

HAPPY NEW YEAR!

SHANAH TOVAH

RUTH IS NEVER BAD

יֶלֶד

BOY

YELED

יוֹם כִּפּוּר

DAY OF ATONEMENT

YOM KIPPUR

יַלְדָּה

GIRL

YALDAH

מוֹרָה

LADY TEACHER

MORAH

בֵּית כְּנֶסֶת

TEMPLE

BET KNESSET

THE SUKKAH AND THE NEW FRIENDS

בַּיִת

HOUSE

BAYIT

לוּלָב

PALM

LULAV

אֶתְרוֹג

CITRON

ETROG

סֻכָּה

BOOTH

SUKKAH

סֻכּוֹת

SUKKOT

SUKKOT

A PRETTY FLAG

דֶּגֶל **DEGEL**

FLAG

רַבִּי

RABBI

RABEE

שִׂמְחַת תּוֹרָה

REJOICING OF THE LAW

SIMHAT TORAH

תּוֹרָה

TORAH

TORAH

חַזָּן

CANTOR

HAZAN

MOSES AND BEZALEL

מֹשֶׁה

MOSES
MOSHEH

עֲשֶׂרֶת הַדִּבְּרוֹת

TEN COMMANDMENTS
ASERET HADIBROT

תּוֹרָה

TORAH
TORAH

מִשְׁכָּן

TABERNACLE
MISHKAN

THE MYSTERY OF THE MISSING CROWN

אֲרוֹן־קֹדֶשׁ

HOLY ARK

ARON KODESH

בֵּית כְּנֶסֶת

TEMPLE

BET KNESSET

רַבִּי

RABBI

RABEE

חַזָּן

CANTOR

HAZAN

תּוֹרָה

TORAH

TORAH

כֶּתֶר

CROWN

KETER

114

SHABBAT SHALOM

שַׁבָּת
SABBATH
SHABBAT

נֵרוֹת
CANDLE
NAYROT

חַלָּה
TWIST BREAD
ḤALLAH

קִדּוּשׁ
SANCTIFICATION
KIDDUSH

שַׁבָּת שָׁלוֹם
GOOD SABBATH!
SHABBAT SHALOM

THE LOST ḤANUKAH TOP

סְבִיבוֹן

DRAYDEL
S'VEEVON

חֲנֻכָּה

FEAST OF LIGHTS
ḤANUKAH

מְנוֹרָה

MENORAH
MENORAH

לְבִיבוֹת

PANCAKES
L'VEEVOT

נ ג ה שׁ

NUN, GIMEL, HAY, SHIN
NUN, GIMMEL, HAY, SHIN

116

A TREE FOR TU B'SHEVAT

פֵּרוֹת

FRUITS

PEROT

יִשְׂרָאֵל

ISRAEL

YISRAEL

עֵץ

TREE

AYTZ

תְּעוּדָה

CERTIFICATE

T'OODAH

טוּ בִּשְׁבָט

NEW YEAR FOR TREES

TU B'SHEVAT

עֵץ

TREE

AYTZ

שָׁלוֹם

HELLO!

GOODBYE!

SHALOM

חוֹנִי

HONI

ḤONI

THE JEWISH WELFARE FUND

סַבְתָּא

GRANDMOTHER

SAVTAH

צְדָקָה

CHARITY

TZ'DAKAH

חֻמָּשׁ

FIVE BOOKS OF MOSES

ḤUMASH

בַּיִת

HOUSE

BAYIT

A PURIM TREAT

מַלְכָּה

QUEEN
MALKAH

מֶלֶךְ

KING
MELEḤ

רַעֲשָׁן   **RAH'AH'SHON**

NOISE MAKER

מְגִלָה

MEGILLAH SCROLL
MEGILLAH

אֹזֶן הָמָן

HAMANTASH-CAKE
OZEN HAMAN

פּוּרִים

FEAST OF LOTS
PURIM
PURIM

QUEEN ESTHER—A PURIM STORY

מְרְדְּכַי

MORDECAI

MORDEHAI

אֶסְתֵּר

ESTHER

ESTHER

אֲחַשְׁוֵרוֹשׁ

AHASUERUS

AHASH'VEROSH

וַשְׁתִּי

VASHTI

VASHTI

פּוּרִים

FEAST OF LOTS

PURIM

הָמָן

HAMAN

HAMAN

BABY MOSES IS A LIVING DOLL

פֶּסַח
PASSOVER
PESAH

הַגָּדָה
HAGGADAH
HAGGADAH

תִּינוֹק
BABY
TEENOK

אִמָּא
MOTHER
EEMAH

מַצָּה
MATZAH
MATZAH

THE BIRTHDAY

בֵּית הַסֵּפֶר

SCHOOL
BET HASEFER

מוֹרָה

LADY TEACHER
MORAH

יִשְׂרָאֵל

ISRAEL
YISRAEL

בַּיִת

HOUSE
BAYIT

A PICNIC FOR LAG B'OMER

לַ"ג בָּעֹמֶר

LAG B'OMER

LAG B'OMER

סֵפֶר

BOOK

SEFER

GLEANINGS FROM THE CORNERS

יִשְׂרָאֵל

ISRAEL
YISRAEL

רוּת

RUTH
RUTH

שָׁבוּעוֹת

FEAST OF WEEKS
SHAVUOT